W0182662

Countryside Musings

Expanded Edition

Countryside Musings – Expanded Edition

Poems written by Jeremy Green

Images supplied by PEXELS and Unsplash

First Printing, 2019

Texte: © Copyright by Jeremy Green
Umschlaggestaltung: © Copyright by Jeremy Green

Verlag: Jeremy Green
jeremygreen@hotmail.de
Eisenbahnstr. 19 42781 Haan Deutschland

Druck: epubli – ein Service der neopubli GmbH, Berlin

Copyright

Copyright © 2019 Jeremy Green

All rights reserved. This book or any portion thereof may not be reproduced or used in any manner whatsoever without the express written permission of the author or publisher except for the use of brief quotations in a book review.

Disclaimer

This is a work of fiction. Names, characters, businesses, places, events, locales, and incidents are either the products of the author's imagination or used in a fictitious manner. Any resemblance to actual persons, living or dead, or actual events is purely coincidental.

Both the author and publisher regret any unintentional harm resulting from the publishing and marketing of this book.

Poems

Rupert

Rupert

Observing from a distance as life went tumbling by
Grazing in his corner on Rupert I would spy
He simply would ignore when others came about
Just a look of slight disdain or the occasional pout
Munching through the endless days on his chosen spot
Seemingly disgruntled with his meagre lot
Then right out of character he'd lift his head to me
And arrange his sheepy features in a smile quite full of glee.

Home

Home

It stood at the end of a long winding road
Surrounded by nature our crumbling abode
The rooms were many and through them we'd roam
The towering edifice we knew as our home

With acres of hills and woodland to search
Willow, oak, chestnut and birch
We'd romp through the summer with no cares to name
For countryside children 'twas always the same

As winter arrived and with it, cold weather
A gloom would descend and we'd huddle together
Into the kitchen, the room we loved most
To warm our chilled flesh with hot tea and toast

The months would drag by and slowly the spring
Would lift up her head and bashfully sing
And with her our battered old house made of stone
Once more became a glorious home.

Bluebell

Bluebell

My favorite time of year produces colours like no other

A meadow of the richest blue between the trees does gather

Exquisite fragile hanging heads scented sweet for cheer

Dancing just to give us pleasure or so it would appear

The velvet carpet they exhibit, a gift from Mother Nature

Is short-lived, but will return with beauty ever greater.

A Village Event

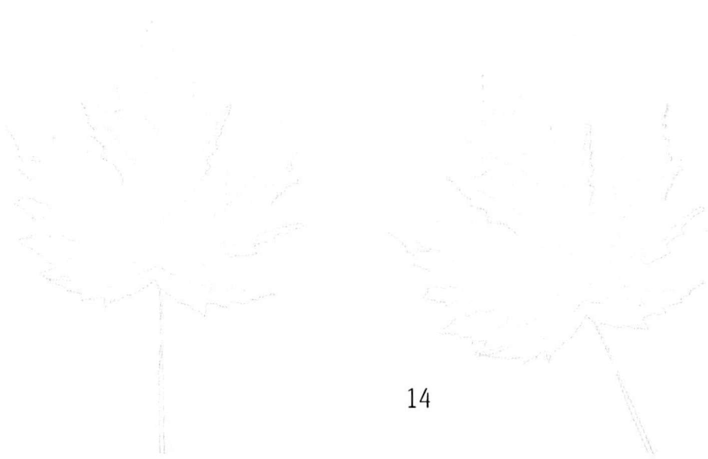

A Village Event

The village green will soon be bustling with crowds of young and old
If you've never been to an English fete here's what you'll behold
The stalls of local arts and crafts have much creative display
Paintings, sketches and decoration in wood, cork and clay

The ladies who bake come out in force with gâteaux, scones and jellies
The husbands indulge, their shirt buttons popping to expose great bulging bellies
For farmers and hobby gardeners alike there's the "Giant Vegetable Event"
With colossal parsnips, beetroots and leeks it's an annual day out well spent

The races are always a main attraction, the competition intense
The potato sack, the egg and spoon are watched with great suspense
There's a bouncy castle, morris dancing, "Splat The Rat" and more
Buttered crumpets, clotted cream and home-made jam galore

Nowhere else, I'm quite convinced will you find such simple cheer
As the time-honored English village fete when it arrives each year.

Old Friend

Old Friend

The day in mid-June was dull as my desire for solace arrived
The country road I'd chosen to walk was silent, dusty and dried
My thoughts were jumbled, my head chaotic as I looked in the distance and spied
My giant old friend crooked and gnarled, his branches of rain deprived
As he stood alone and my approach hastened returned the solace I'd cried
My longing was stilled as I rested beneath him, my body and spirit revived.

Beaches of England

Beaches of England

The beaches of England, some really first rate
Were a joy as a child on the holidays we'd take
The car well-stocked, the caravan we'd haul
Along country lanes we'd move at a crawl

Arriving at night, we children disgruntled
We'd fall in to bed exhausted and rumpled
At the first sign of day we'd charge out of bed
Thrilled at the thought of what lay ahead

With fishing nets, spades and buckets brimming
We'd spend the days hunting, laughing and swimming
The weeks flying by, full of childhood pleasure
We'd return home with gigantic bags full of treasure

Quickly our thoughts of adventure would fade
Till a full year had passed and new plans were laid
The beaches of England are really first rate
A wondrous joy on the holidays we'd take.

The Flight

The Flight

Look right, look left; it's time to decide
To risk the run, or rather to hide
Between us the space is increasingly wide

My mate before me I see

My senses today help not a lot
My panic increases, I'm glued to the spot
The hounds it seems, for blood they are hot

My mate ever further from me

My indecision must come to an end
I pray that the dash may be my best friend
The flight I take is rapid to end

My mate lies next to me.

Autumn's Game

Autumn's Game

Caught on the wind, my friends next to me

Swiftly we race with a turbulent glee

The weather has turned, the summer departed

Our journey together is lively, lighthearted

I glance below; on the ground others lie

For me there's no lull, I continue to fly

Suddenly my speed is sluggish at best

My excitement has dimmed, I'm longing for rest

Then in an instant I'm off once again

For a leaf has no choice, this is autumn's game.

The Squirrel

The Squirrel

Quick darting movements

Time to rest, never

Eyes ever searching

Vulnerable, clever

His coat shines red

A glimmer through the trees

An instant in view

Then gone like the breeze.

Sunday Mornings

Sunday Mornings

Early sunday mornings off to Church we'd go
Greeted by the Vicar with a big cheery "Hello"
The village in its entirety, dolled up to be seen
Farmers, housewives and we kids looking so serene

The Hymns we sang with vigour, tuneless though we were
The organist her timing off, slowing to a slur
Mother would leave early still singing as she parted
Rushing off towards the house to get the cooking started

As church would end we'd wander home guessing what's for lunch
Pork and roast potatoes with crackling to crunch?
We'd eat, we'd drink, we'd chat away, we kids would usually fight
Then stumble to a comfy chair collapsing with delight

Dad would wash, mum would doze, all happy in our way
Our lovely sunday mornings, great memories they will stay.

Pink Lady

Pink Lady

My life began in gorgeous green

With pink I was lady and I was queen

When yellow arrived my age was on show

With brown came my fall and the end of the road.

Winter Ride

Winter Ride

A burning sensation in my nose appears
Then a slight numbness of lips and ears
As my speed increases its hard not to see
My hands turn a colour they should not be
With my legs bent up, knees under chin
Each part of my body knows the trouble it's in
My mother was right, as all now can see
Tobogganing naked just isn't for me.

Countryside Musings

Expanded Edition

With many thanks for their invaluable help and encouragement

Jan, Betty, Lars, Debbie and Paul

ISBN 978-3-7485-0553-2
9 783748 505532 00001
www.epubli.de